James
the Red

Based on *The Railway Series* by the Rev. W. Awdry

Illustrations by *Robin Davies and Creative Design*

EGMONT

EGMONT

We bring stories to life

First published in Great Britain 2003
This edition published in 2011
by Egmont UK Limited
The Yellow Building, 1 Nicholas Road, London W11 4AN

Thomas the Tank Engine & Friends™

CREATED BY BRITT ALLCROFT

HiT entertainment

ISBN 978 1 4052 6960 5
42110/44
Printed in Italy

Stay safe online. Egmont is not responsible for content hosted by third parties.

FSC
MIX
Paper
FSC® C018306

Egmont is passionate about helping to preserve the world's remaining ancient forests. We only use paper from legal and sustainable forest sources.

This book is made from paper certified by the Forest Stewardship Council® (FSC®), an organisation dedicated to promoting responsible management of forest resources. For more information on the FSC, please visit www.fsc.org. To learn more about Egmont's sustainable paper policy, please visit www.egmont.co.uk/ethical

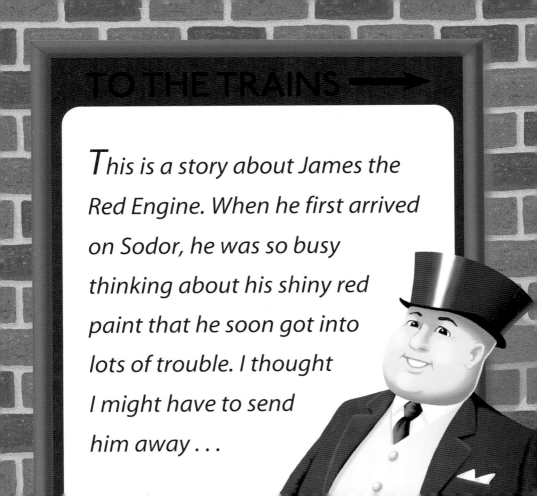

This is a story about James the Red Engine. When he first arrived on Sodor, he was so busy thinking about his shiny red paint that he soon got into lots of trouble. I thought I might have to send him away . . .

James was a new engine, with a shining coat of red paint. He had two small wheels in front and six driving wheels behind. They were smaller than Gordon's, but bigger than Thomas'.

"You're a special 'mixed traffic' engine," The Fat Controller told James. "That means you can pull either coaches or trucks."

James felt very proud.

The Fat Controller told James that today he was to help Edward pull coaches.

"You need to be careful with coaches," said Edward. "They don't like getting bumped. If you bump them, they'll get cross."

But James was thinking about his shiny red coat and wasn't really listening.

James and Edward took the coaches to the platform. A group of boys came over to admire James.

"I really am a splendid engine," thought James, and he let out a great *wheeeeeesh* of steam. Everyone jumped, and a shower of water fell on The Fat Controller, soaking his brand new top hat!

James thought he had better leave quickly before he got into trouble, so he pulled away from the platform.

"Slow down!" puffed Edward, who didn't like starting quickly.

"You're going too fast, you're going too fast," grumbled the coaches.

When James reached the next station, he shot past the platform. His Driver had to back up so the passengers could get off the train.
"The Fat Controller won't be pleased when he hears about this," his Driver said.

James and Edward set off again, and started to climb a hill. "It's ever so steep, it's ever so steep," puffed James.

At last they got to the top, and pulled into the next station. James was panting so much that he got hiccups, and frightened an old lady, who dropped all her parcels.

"Oh, dear. The Fat Controller will be even crosser, now!" thought James.

The next morning, The Fat Controller spoke to James very sternly. "If you don't learn to behave better, I shall take away your red coat and paint you blue!" he warned. "Now run along and fetch your coaches."

James felt cross. "A splendid red engine like me shouldn't have to fetch his own coaches," he muttered.

"I'll show them how to pull coaches," he said to himself, and he set off at top speed. The coaches groaned and protested as they bumped along. But James wouldn't slow down.

At last, the coaches had had enough. "We're going to stop, we're going to stop!" they cried, and try as he might, James found himself going slower and slower.

The Driver halted the train and got out. "There's a leak in the pipe," he said. "You were bumping the coaches hard enough to make a leak in anything!"

The Guard made all the passengers get out of the train. "You sir, please give me your bootlace," he said to one of them.

"No, I shan't!" said the passenger.

"Well then, we shall just have to stop where we are," said the Guard.

So the man agreed to give his bootlace to the Guard. The Guard used the lace to tie a pad of newspapers round the hole to stop the leak.

Now James was able to pull the train again. But he knew he was going to be in real trouble with The Fat Controller this time.

When James got back, The Fat Controller was very angry with him indeed.

For the next few days, James was left alone in the shed in disgrace. He wasn't even allowed to push coaches and trucks in the Yard.

He felt really sad.

Then one morning, The Fat Controller came to see him. "I see you are sorry," he said to James. "So I'd like you to pull some trucks for me."

"Thank you, Sir!" said James, and he puffed happily away.

"Here are your trucks, James," said a little engine. "Have you got some bootlaces ready?" And he chuffed off, laughing rudely.

"Oh! Oh! Oh!" said the trucks as James backed down on them. "We want a proper engine, not a Red Monster."

James took no notice, but pulled the screeching trucks out of the Yard.

James started to heave the trucks up the hill, puffing and panting.

But halfway up, the last ten trucks broke away and rolled back down again. James' Driver shut off steam. "We'll have to go back and get them," he said to James.

James backed carefully down the hill to collect the trucks. Then with a 'peep peep' he was off again.

"I can do it, I can do it," he puffed, then … "I've done it, I've done it," he panted as he climbed over the top.

When James got back to the station, The Fat Controller was very pleased with him. "You've made the most Troublesome Trucks on the line behave," he said. "After that, you deserve to keep your red coat!"

James was really happy. He knew he was going to enjoy working on The Fat Controller's Railway!